MORE!

EMMA CHICHESTER CLARK

PictureLions

An Imprint of HarperCollins*Publishers*

First published in Great Britain by Andersen Press Ltd in 1998.
First published in Picture Lions in 1999.
3 5 7 9 10 8 6 4 2
ISBN: 0 00 664672 7
Picture Lions is an imprint of the Children's Division, part of HarperCollins Publishers Ltd,
77–85 Fulham Palace Road, Hammersmith, London W6 8JB.
Text and illustrations copyright © Emma Chichester Clark 1998.
The author/illustrator asserts the moral right to be identified as the author/illustrator of the work.
The HarperCollins website address is: www.**fire**and**water**.com
Printed and bound in Singapore by Imago.

"One more game of hide-and-seek," said Billy.

So they played another.

"More!" said Billy.

"Just one more," said his mother.

"More!" said Billy.

"That's enough!" said his mother.

"One more story," said Billy. So his mother read another.

"More!" said Billy.

"Just one more," said his mother.

"More!" said Billy.

"That's enough!" said his mother.

"One more ice-cream," said Billy. So he had another.

"More!" said Billy.

"Just one more," said his mother.

"More!" said Billy.

"That's enough!" said his mother.

"I've had enough of YOU!" Billy shouted,
and he stomped up the stairs.

"It's not fair!" Billy told
the lion who lived behind
the curtain.
"Tell me all about it,"
said the lion.
So Billy told him.

"I know a place where there is
more of everything," said the lion.
"As much as I like?" asked Billy.
"More than you could ever want,"
said the lion. "Close your eyes and
I'll take you there."

And then they were flying
and whooshing and soaring.
"More!" cried Billy. "More, more, more!"

"There is more," said the lion. "Look!"
Billy opened his eyes, and there it was...

They whizzed
down the
whirligig...

MORE!

...and spun around the spindletops...

"More!" cried Billy,
as they hooted through
the harum scarum.

"More!" cried Billy,
as they hurtled up
the hullabaloo.

"More!" cried Billy,
as they looped
around the loop.

"More!" shouted Billy to the booming of the drums.

There was crackling and crashing, banging and bashing.

There were running races, leaping races,

bouncing and balancing,

hopping and jumping and prizes for winning.

Then there was eating
and licking
and chomping,
through forests
of lollies...

and fields of sweet
flowers...

And then there was MORE stomping,
MORE leaping, MORE romping...
"More?" asked the lion.
"Well..." whispered Billy.

"No more lollies?" asked the lion.
"No more," whispered Billy.
"No more racing?" asked the lion.
"No more," whispered Billy.
"No more spinning?" asked the lion.
"No more," murmured Billy.

"No more of anything?" asked the lion.
"No, that's enough," answered Billy,
and he yawned a great yawn.

And the lion said, "BED!"

"I can't sleep," whispered Billy, but nobody heard him.
"I need my mum and my very own bed."

And that's when he heard her.
"Billy, where are you?"

"I'm coming!" cried Billy. He ran through the forest

and under the spindletops, faster and faster...

He raced like the wind.
Then he stumbled... he toppled...

He started to tumble...

over, and over,

flying and falling...

"There you are!" said his mother.

She kissed him and hugged him
and then she said, "More!"
"Just one more," said Billy.
"More!" said his mother.
"That's enough!" laughed Billy.

"I'll NEVER have enough of YOU!"
smiled his mother, and she turned off
the light.